APOLLO 13

The Movie Storybook

This is a drawing of the Apollo spacecraft—just like the one in **Apollo 13.**

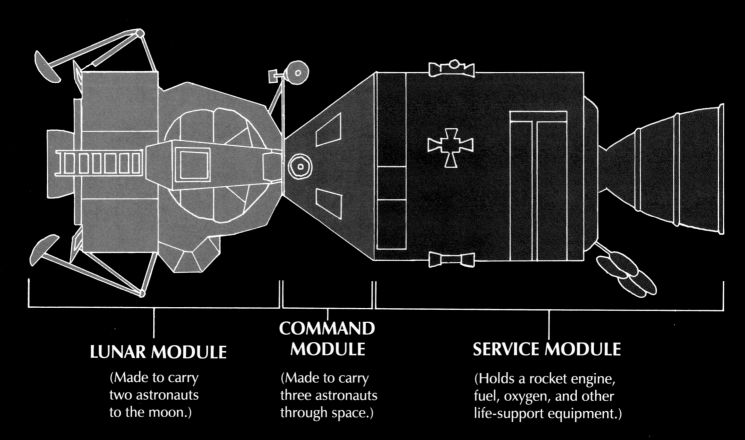

LUNAR MODULE

(Made to carry
two astronauts
to the moon.)

COMMAND MODULE

(Made to carry
three astronauts
through space.)

SERVICE MODULE

(Holds a rocket engine,
fuel, oxygen, and other
life-support equipment.)

Library of Congress Cataloging-in-Publication Data
Mason, Jane B. Apollo 13 : the movie storybook / adapted by Jane B. Mason ; screenplay by William Broyles, Jr. & Al Reinert and John Sayles.   p.   cm.   "With photos from NASA and the movie Apollo 13. Based on the book Lost Moon by Jim Lovell and Jeffrey Kluger."
1. Apollo 13 (Spacecraft)—Accidents—Juvenile literature.   2. Space vehicle accidents—United States—Juvenile literature.   [1. Apollo 13 (Spacecraft)   2. Project Apollo (U.S.)   3. Space vehicle accidents.]   I. Title.   TL789.8.U6A5553   1995   791.43'72—dc20   95-13068
CIP   AC

ISBN 0-448-41119-9   A B C D E F G H I J

Official Apollo 13 emblem
and photos on page 14 and 28 courtesy of NASA.

APOLLO 13

The Movie Storybook

Adapted by **Jane B. Mason**

From a motion picture written by
William Broyles, Jr. & Al Reinert and John Sayles

Based on the book *Lost Moon* by
Jim Lovell and Jeffrey Kluger

Grosset & Dunlap

New York

Commander Jim Lovell took a step on a grayish, barren landscape. Dust swirled around his feet. The sun was blinding, but the face shield on his helmet protected him from its harsh rays. Leaning forward, he picked up a piece of rock with a giant mechanical scoop.

Beside him, astronaut Fred Haise awkwardly hoisted his own scoop. "This thing is going to be a lot easier to handle when there's no gravity," he said.

Jim smiled. These men weren't walking on the moon—yet. They were walking on a simulated moon landscape at NASA's Mission Control Headquarters in Houston, Texas. But they *were* getting ready for the voyage of a lifetime. Apollo 13. In just a few days, Jim, Fred, and their crewmate Ken Mattingly would ride a rocket ship into space and Jim and Fred would walk on the moon.

Jim, Ken, and Fred had spent the last few months together training for their mission. Now their trip was just one week away.

But two days before takeoff, the flight surgeon approached Jim. He had bad news. One of the Apollo backup pilots had the measles. That meant the whole crew had been exposed.

Jim shrugged. "So, I've had the measles."

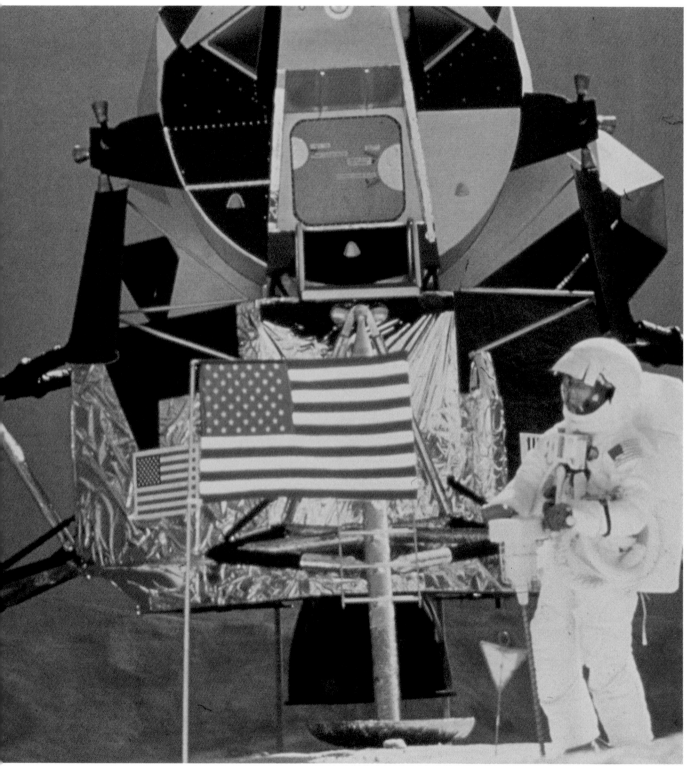

But his command module pilot, Ken Mattingly, hadn't. "Either we dump Ken Mattingly and go with the back-up pilot Jack Swigert," the doctor said, "or we bump all of you."

It was a difficult choice. Jack Swigert was good. He was young and eager and smart. But he was also inexperienced. He had never flown on a space mission before. Ken Mattingly knew the spaceship inside and out. Still, Jim knew if his whole crew was bumped now, there was a good chance that they would never get to go on another mission.

The decision was made. Ken was grounded. Now they just had to get Jack Swigert ready. For the next two days, Jack would have to spend long hours in the rocket simulator with Jim and Fred. He had forty-eight hours to catch up with their months of training.

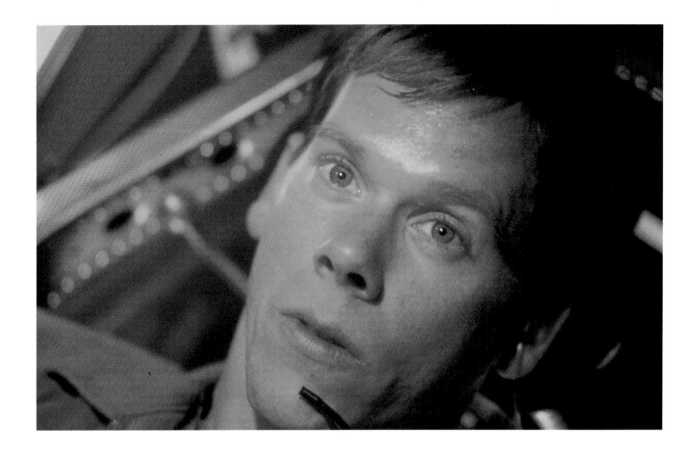

Jack's first session in the simulator was not encouraging. The astronauts were practicing the final maneuver of the mission: reentering the earth's atmosphere. It would be Jack's job to steer the command module—the astronauts' mother ship—back home. And it had to be done exactly right. If the ship came in too shallow, it would skip off the atmosphere and bounce back into space—forever. If it came in too steep, the ship would reenter too quickly and be burned up by the friction—along with the men inside.

Jack thought they were coming in too shallow. "I'm going to manual," he announced calmly.

Then, suddenly, the g-force indicator veered right.

"Twelve g's! We're in too steep!" yelled Jack.

"Twelve g's?" said Jim. "We're burning up."

WAH!-WAH!-WAH!-WAH! The mission failure alarm went off around them. Twelve g's of force was more than any human being or spaceship could stand.

As Jim stepped out of the simulator, he had to wonder if he'd made the right decision. Could Jack do the job?

NASA's chief astronaut, Deke Slayton, wondered too. "So?" he asked Jim. "Is this going to work?"

Jim nodded. "He made a common mistake," said Jim. "He won't make it again." Jim was determined. "We've got two days. He'll be ready." *He's got to be*, Jim thought.

By launch day, Jack was. On April 11, 1970, he was certified fit to fly and introduced as the new pilot of the Apollo 13 mission.

At the Launch Center in Cape Kennedy, Florida, the Apollo 13 spacecraft stood ready to go. At 1:13—thirteen hundred hours and thirteen minutes, military time—it would be rocketed into space. On April 13, it would be in the moon's field of gravity—and be on its way to landing on the moon.

Some people worried that all those thirteens would bring the mission bad luck. But the astronauts were too excited to worry about silly superstitions. In a large, sterile room called the suit room, technicians helped them put on the bulky white pressure suits, gloves, and fish-bowl-shaped helmets that would protect them in space.

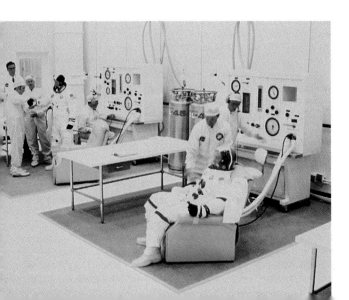

Once they were dressed, the crew was transported to the launchpad, where an elevator carried them up the 363-foot-tall Saturn 5 rocket—the engine that would carry them into space. They climbed into the command module, and minutes later they were strapped into their seats.

The hatch was lowered.

They were ready to go.

At Mission Control in Houston, giant charts and graphs lit up the walls. Controllers were busy at their computers, making sure everything was in order. As soon as the rocket cleared the launchpad, they would take over control of Apollo 13 from the Launch Center in Florida.

The flight director of the first control team, Gene Kranz, slipped into his signature white vest and put on his headphones. "Launch Control," he said, "this is Houston. We are go for launch."

Back in Florida, the astronauts' friends, families, and fans stood by along with news crews from around the world. Over the loudspeaker, an announcer spoke to the crowd of spectators. "Apollo 13 is go for launch in one minute thirty seconds."

A second later, the crowd began to chant—softly and slowly at first, getting louder and faster as the seconds ticked by. "Go! Go! Go! Go!"

And then, "Ten, nine, eight . . ."

The command module hummed as pumps filled the fuel tanks.

"Seven, six, five . . ."

"Get ready for the kickoff, fellas," Jim said.

"Four, three, two, one . . ."

A volcano of flame erupted downward from the engines as an ear-splitting roar filled the air . . . and Apollo 13 soared into the sky.

Two and a half minutes later, thirty-eight miles above the earth, the sky outside the cockpit was a deep, dark blue. The huge first stage of the rocket fell away, and the astronauts braced themselves for another enormous jolt as the five second stage engines came on. But on the control panel, one of the engine lights was fading.

"Houston, we've got a center engine cut-off," Jim said, trying to sound calm.

"Roger that, 13. We've got the same," Mission Control replied.

Jim looked at the "ABORT" button on the control panel. Would Mission Control tell him to push it and turn the ship around? The astronauts waited.

Gene Kranz took off his headphones and looked over at his engineers. "Is this a problem?" he asked.

"As long as we don't lose another engine," one replied, "we'll be alright."

At last the astronauts' radio cackled back to life. "We're not sure why the engine went out early, 13, but you are *GO*. We'll just burn the other four engines a little longer."

Jim let out a relieved sigh. "Looks like we've had our glitch for this mission," he said.

Two minutes later, they were in outer space!

The first two days of the voyage went exactly as planned. On the night of day three, the Apollo 13 astronauts even delivered a television broadcast from space. Jim's wife Marilyn and their children gathered with the other astronauts' families in the Mission Control viewing room to watch it.

Suddenly, the screen at the back of the room came to life, and Jim's smiling face greeted the camera. "Welcome to Apollo 13," he said. "We're coming to you live from an altitude of almost 200,000 miles away from Earth. Tonight we're going to show you what we do up here in outer space."

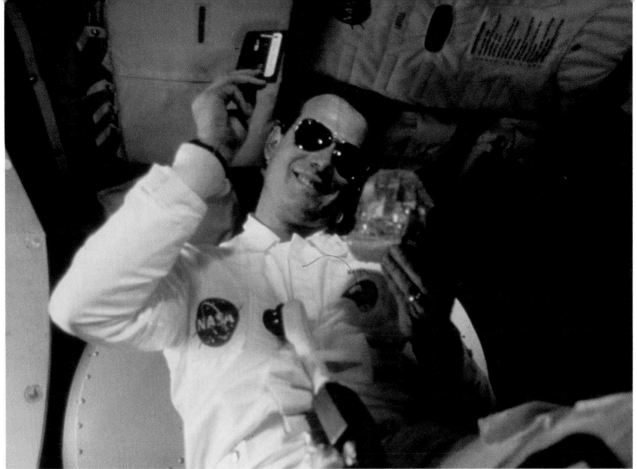

Suddenly Fred came on-screen, wearing aviator glasses and holding a cassette player and tape. "How 'bout a little background music," he said, grinning. He slipped the tape in and a rock song came on.

Then Jim gave a tour of the lunar module, which the crew had named *Aquarius*. That was the spacecraft that would take Jim and Fred down to the moon's surface while Jack waited in the command module. They had named this ship the *Odyssey*, a word which means "long voyage."

"The lunar module is connected by this little tunnel here," Jim explained as he and Fred "swam" through the passage into the lunar module. "The lunar module is about the size of two telephone booths," he explained. "Right now we're separated from the vacuum of space by a layer only as thick as three pieces of aluminum foil." After all, the lunar module was not the kind of craft you stayed in for long. It was built to make the short trip from the *Odyssey* to the moon and back—and that was all.

A few minutes later, Jim signed off. "This is the crew of Apollo 13," he said, "wishing everyone on Earth a nice evening."

"Nice show," Mission Control radioed up as soon as the astronauts were off the air. "Now we've got a couple of housekeeping chores for you to do. Could you give the oxygen tanks a stir?"

"Roger that," Jack replied. From his seat he reached for the switch that would stir the tanks of concentrated oxygen slush stored in the service module. Like the trunk of a car, the service module rode behind the command module, where it carried such spaceship essentials as fuel, life-support equipment, and part of the engine. Stirring the oxygen tanks was a routine procedure. It kept the gas flowing through the fuel cells where it could be turned into electricity, water, and heat for the ship.

With a flick of his finger, Jack flipped the switch.

BANG! A loud explosion rocked the spaceship. A second later the ship started to shake. The "CREW ALERT" signal blinked on the control panel.

"Houston—" Jim tried to keep his voice steady as the ship lurched from side to side like a knuckleball. "—we have a problem."

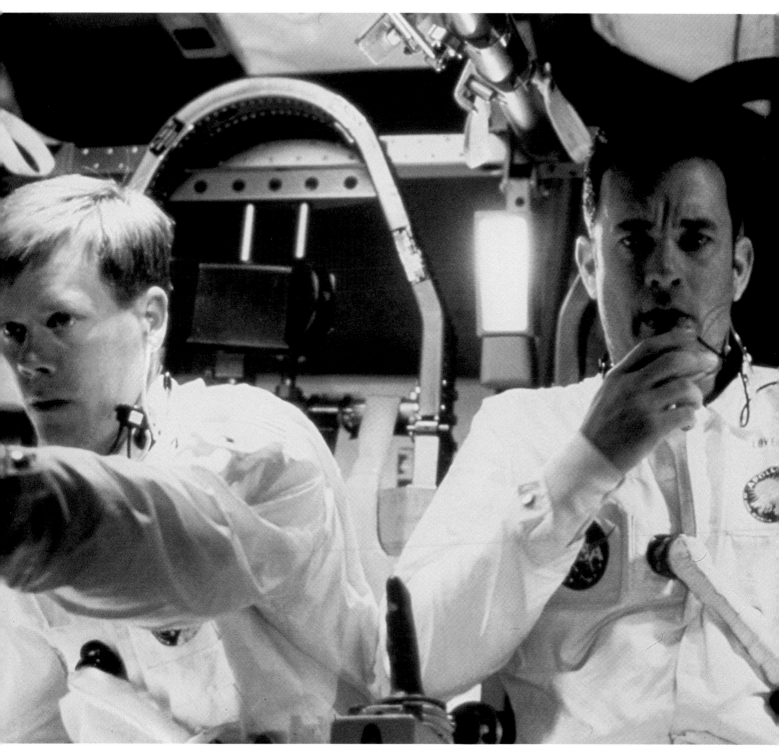

At Mission Control, the engineers stared at their computer screens.

"Oxygen tank one not reading," a controller said.

"I keep losing radio signal!" exclaimed another.

In space, Jim floated over to the window and looked out. A cloud of crystals surrounded the ship, leaving a trail for miles.

"Uh, Houston, it looks like we're venting something," he said. "It's a gas of some sort. It's got to be oxygen. . . ."

Venting oxygen! As horrible as that was, Gene Kranz knew that Jim's guess had to be right. Without oxygen, the astronauts would have nothing—no heat, no power, no air. They had to do something—and fast!

"Okay people." Kranz looked around at his controllers. "We're moving the astronauts over to the lunar module. We need to power it up and shut down the command module at the same time. The *Aquarius* just became a lifeboat."

The lunar module had its own power and oxygen supplies. With its thin walls and no heat shield, it could not reenter the earth's atmosphere, but it could buy the astronauts some time.

"Exactly how much time do we have, Houston?" Jim asked.

There was a pause. "We're looking at less than fifteen minutes of life support left in the *Odyssey*," Kranz replied.

Fifteen minutes! They would have to transfer all power and computer information to the lunar module in fifteen minutes. Could they do it? It was an incredible long shot . . . .

And it was the only shot they had.

While Houston gave him instructions over the radio, Jack worked on powering down the injured command module.

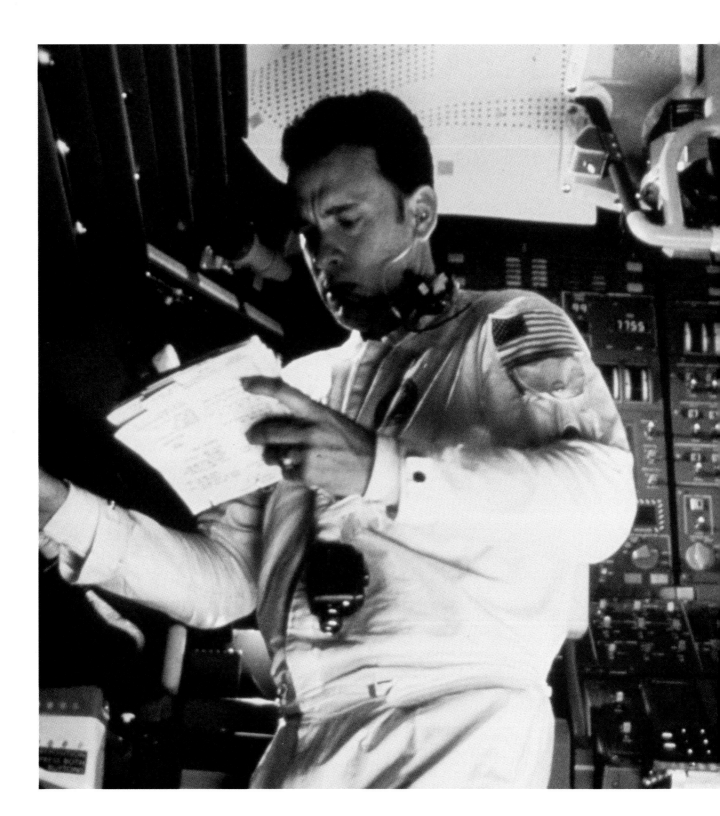

Meanwhile, Jim and Fred hurried to get the lunar module up and running.

Ten minutes later, Jack reached for the last switch. "Houston, I have powered down. I have no control left. I am turning my engines off."

Jack looked around his darkened ship. "Do we know for sure that we can power this thing back up?" he asked. "It's gonna get awful cold in here." But there was no answer, so he hit the final "OFF" button.

Outside the ship, the temperature could fall as low as 280 degrees below zero. Left without power for several days, the command module was sure to freeze. They would have to use it again to reenter the earth's atmosphere. Would they be able to? There would be only one way to find out.

Within hours, newscasters around the world were making the public aware of Apollo 13's plight—and the engineers at Mission Control were working on the solution.

As soon as a new shift of controllers arrived, Gene Kranz assembled his first team of engineers in a conference room to plan.

"So how do we get our people home?" Kranz asked. He turned to a blackboard and drew two circles—the moon and the earth. Four-fifths of the way from the earth to the moon, he drew an X. "They're here," he said, pointing to the X. "Now all we have to do is bring them back.

"I think our only option is to use the moon's gravity to slingshot them around—" Kranz drew a line circling behind the moon. "—and shoot them back to Earth."

Several engineers nodded. It was the only way.

"But the lunar module isn't designed to support three men for that long!" one controller objected.

"I don't care what it was *designed* to do," said Kranz. "I care about what it *can* do."

It was day four of the journey and Apollo 13 had reached the moon. Soon it would disappear behind it.

"We're going to lose contact with you for twenty-eight minutes," Mission Control radioed.

"Roger," Jim replied as the planet Earth drifted out of view.

For the next half hour, the astronauts coasted through black nothingness—nothing but dark, eerie silence—behind the dark side of the moon.

Then, suddenly, a long arc of sun peeked over the rugged curve of the moon. Fred and Jack crowded by the small window and looked down at the gray, dusty surface just sixty miles below them.

"Wow! Look at that!" Fred exclaimed. He snapped a picture.

"It's a beautiful sight," Jack agreed. "Jim, you've got to see this."

But Jim wasn't interested in the moon at the moment. He'd seen it already, when he flew on Apollo 8. This time he was supposed to have touched the moon. Now, Jim thought, he would be lucky if he touched the earth again.

By now, every corridor and console of Mission Control was teeming with engineers. As new people came on duty, exhausted controllers tried to rest. But in the conference room, Gene Kranz was still at work, dealing with the next matter of business: How to get the astronauts home. The lunar module was designed to carry two men for a day and a half. How could it support three men for the three days it would take to travel from the moon to Earth?

"Power is everything," a young electrical officer named John Arthur said. "Without it they can't talk to us—they can't correct their course. Right now they're using sixty amps of power. At that rate their batteries will be dead in less than a day. We've got to get them down to twelve amps if they're going to make it for three more days."

"You can't run a vacuum cleaner on twelve amps!" someone argued.

But Arthur stood firm. "We've got to turn everything off," he said. "Radars . . . the cabin heater . . . even the guidance computer. . . ."

Kranz looked Arthur in the eye. "Okay," he said. "We'll power it down. In the meantime, we've got a frozen command module up there. I want to know how to power it back up."

By the next day, things in the lunar module were looking grim. With nearly all the power off in the tiny ship, the temperature was freezing. The men were exhausted. And now Fred was running a fever.

Fred forced down a couple of dry aspirin and picked up his "Personal Preference Kit." Each astronaut had one to hold photos, letters, and other momentos from home while they were away. As Fred opened the package, his wife's picture floated up in front of him.

"That's a nice picture of Mary," Jim said, coming up behind Fred. But he knew they were really thinking the same thing: *Would they ever see their families again?*

Suddenly a whine like a smoke detector made the astronauts start. They had been so busy worrying about making it home, they hadn't noticed how high the carbon dioxide level had risen.

The lunar module was only designed to filter the carbon dioxide exhaled by two men for a day and a half. Now, after cleaning the carbon dioxide exhaled by three men for over twenty-four hours, the lunar module's built-in air filters were clogging up.

In the cold cabin air, the astronauts could see their breath—breath that could kill them if it was not cleaned.

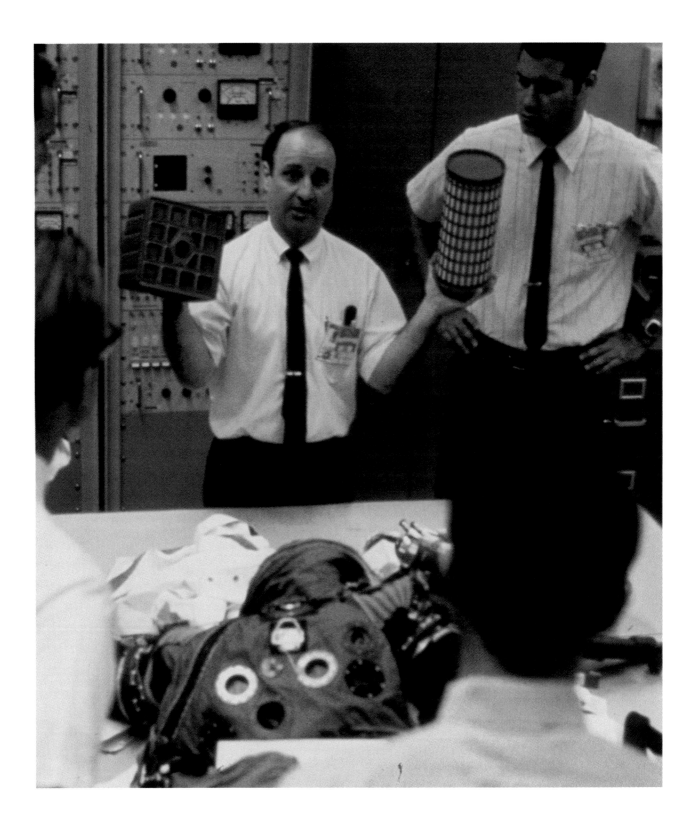

Jim picked up the radio. "Uh, Houston, we have a carbon dioxide reading of thirteen here," he said.

"We were expecting that, *Aquarius*," Houston replied.

"It's comforting to know that," Jim snapped. "Now what do we do about it?"

In fact, Mission Controllers had been up all night trying to build an adapter that would allow the command module's extra square filters to fit into the lunar module's round holes. Of course, they could only use what the astronauts had on board—hoses, tape, cardboard, food bags—anything they could find.

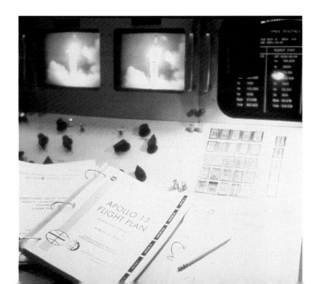

"We've got it!" an engineer finally shouted.

"We've got some things for you to do, *Aquarius*," Mission Control said over the radio. "First, rip the cover off the Flight Plan."

Jack grinned. "With pleasure," he said.

While Houston radioed instructions for assembling the adapter, the astronauts gathered parts.

"I need a sock," Fred said.

"A sock?" Jack asked.

"A sock," Fred repeated. "You know. Foot, shoe, sock. Now, what did you say I should do with this garment bag, Houston?" Fred asked.

Piece by piece, the astronauts put together the air filter adapter. Then they taped it to the outlet in the lunar module's side. When the filter was secured in place, Jack put his ear against it.

"I can hear air moving," he said.

The astronauts turned to look at the carbon dioxide gauge. The alarm was still going off. Then, suddenly, the whine stopped and the needle began to drop.

"Breathe normal, fellas," Jim said with a grin.

The adapter worked.

Now the engineers in Houston were working on yet another problem: reentry. How were they going to power the command module back up with virtually no power?

Luckily, Ken Mattingly had not gotten the measles. He knew the command module better than anyone, and if there was a way to get the ship going, he would figure it out.

Ken strode into the control room, ready to take charge. "Okay, I need the simulator cold and dark. Give me the same conditions those astronauts have now. Let's get this show on the road."

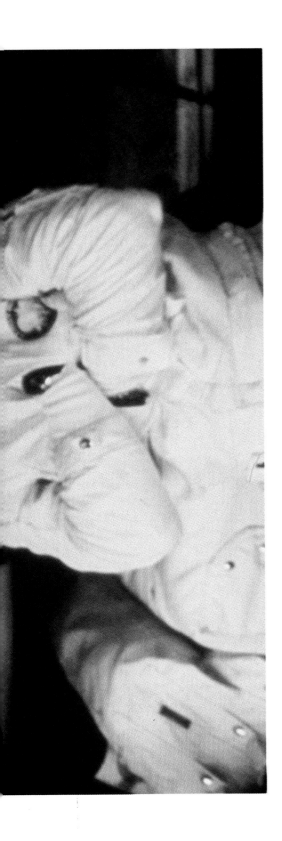

By day seven, the ship was a mess. Food packets and other debris floated around the cabin. The crew still hadn't slept. And Fred's fever had gotten worse. The astronauts were just hours from Earth. But the command module was still frozen. Mission Control had not told them how to power it back up.

"They don't know how to do it," Jack said.

Fred nodded. "Maybe Jack's right."

Jim radioed down to Mission Control. "Houston, we could sure use some instructions for reentry procedure up here," he said impatiently.

But help was slow in coming. It was hours before Ken was in the control room slipping on a headset. "*Aquarius*, this is Houston," he said. "Jack, get yourself into the command module and get something to write on. It's time to power that baby back up."

Jack sat alone in the dark, icy stillness of the dead command module. He was exhausted and his whole body ached. But they were almost home.

Over the radio, Ken called out instructions. "Find the main breakers on panel eleven," he said, "and turn breaker five on."

Jack looked at the instrument panel. Beads of condensed water covered the cold surface. "There's an awful lot of condensation," he said worriedly. "What's the word on these things shorting out?"

Ken knew that the ship's wires were coated with plastic to keep them dry. But if a single drop of water got through a crack or seam, the whole electrical system would short out and be ruined.

"We'll take them one at a time, Jack," Ken said confidently.

"It's like driving a toaster through a car wash," Jack muttered.

Jack reached a shaky hand over to the first switch. Holding his breath, he flipped it on. No short. Jack sighed with relief. "Breaker five on," he said.

Jack smiled and flipped the next switch. Little by little, the astronauts worked their way through the emergency power-up manual and the lights in the cockpit of the mother ship returned. Jack's ship was coming back!

"We got her back up, Ken," said Jack at last. "Wish you were here to see it."

"I'll bet you do," Ken said. "Now, if you're ready, I think it's time to prepare for service module separation."

At last it was time to break free from the useless weight Apollo 13 had been toting through space for the last four days: the service module.

"We're set for jettison!" Jack called to his crewmates back in the lunar module.

"Roger that," Jim said. "On a three count. One, two . . ."

Jack hit the switch to release the service module. "We're loose!" he called.

"There it is!" Fred exclaimed, looking out the lunar module's window. "I see it!"

Jim's jaw dropped as the service module rolled past them in slow motion, revealing a gaping black hole in its side. Broken wires and hoses spewed from the opening like robotic intestines.

"A whole side of the spacecraft is missing," Jim reported to Mission Control. "It's really a mess."

No one could say it, but everyone was thinking the same thing. The service module had fit over the command module's heat shield. What if the explosion had damaged the heat shield too? If it had, the ship would burn up when it tried to reenter the earth's atmosphere ... and so would the astronauts. . . .

In just an hour, Apollo 13 would hit the earth's atmosphere. It was now time to officially leave the ship that had safely carried the astronauts hundreds of thousands of miles. Like the service module, the lunar module too would be cast off into space.

"Jim," Jack called from the pilot seat of the command module. "We're coming up on lunar module jettison."

Jim and Fred took a final look around the *Aquarius,* then floated down the tunnel to the command module and slammed shut the hatch that joined the two ships.

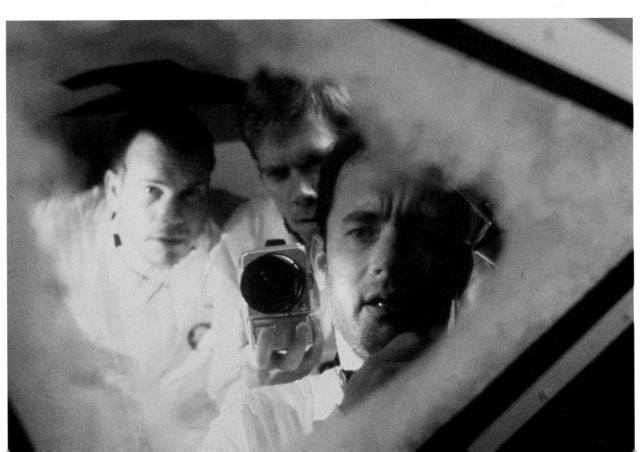

When the men were strapped in, Jack hit another button. With a tiny poof of air, the lunar module separated from the command module. The men watched the spidery craft drift off into space with just a little sadness.

"Farewell, *Aquarius*." Ken's voice came in over the radio. "And we thank you."

A few minutes later, Ken made an announcement to the crew at Mission Control. "We have loss of radio signal. Expect to regain contact in three min-utes." Apollo 13 had hit the earth's atmosphere.

On board, the astronauts were stony as the command module picked up speed. Would the heat shield protect them from the intense friction of the atmosphere? They would know in a matter of seconds.

In the South Pacific, where the *Odyssey* was expected to splash down, sailors on the aircraft carrier *Iwo Jima* scanned the horizon with binoculars.

In the Lovell house, Jim's family waited silently for word.

And at Mission Control, Gene Kranz and the other controllers watched the monitor at the front of the control room and listened for the radio to come back to life.

Three minutes passed.

"*Odyssey*," Ken called, "this is Houston. Do you read?"

There was no answer.

Four minutes passed. Still there was nothing.

Then, suddenly, somebody spotted it. A silvery object falling swiftly toward Earth! The next thing they knew, huge orange parachutes unfolded, and Apollo 13 floated gently down.

The Lovell house . . . the *Iwo Jima* . . . Mission Control . . . the whole world! . . . erupted in cheers.

"Hello, Houston, this is *Odyssey*," Jim said over the radio. "Good to see you again."

Minutes later, the *Odyssey* hit the water. Helicopters from the recovery ship, *Iwo Jima*, hovered over the spacecraft. Divers opened the hatch and lifted the astronauts from the cockpit.

Another cheer rang out as the helicopter touched down on the deck of the aircraft carrier and the Apollo 13 astronauts emerged, weak but smiling.

They were sick. They were filthy. They were exhausted. But they were safe. And they were home.